Two Tails on the Trail

Harry's Dragon Tales, Book 2

Lisa Reinicke

Copyright © 2021 Lisa Reinicke

All rights reserved.

No part of this publication in print or in electronic format may be reproduced, stored in a retrieval system, or transmitted in any form or by any means, electronic, mechanical, photocopying, recording, or otherwise without the prior written permission of the publisher.

This is a work of fiction. Names, characters, organizations, places, events and incidents are either the products of the author's imagination or are used fictitiously. Any resemblance to actual persons, living or dead, or actual events is purely coincidental.

Edited by Kathy Meis
Cover Art by Analise Black
Published by One House Publications, LLC

ISBN: 978-1-647042-79-0 Paperback
ISBN: 978-1-647042-78-3 eBook

Library of Congress Number: 2020923982

TABLE OF CONTENTS

Chapter 1: A Smoking Egg 1

Chapter 2: Yay to Stay! 9

Chapter 3: Manners and Munchies 17

Chapter 4: Marching Onward 27

Chapter 5: Hangry Harry 37

Chapter 6: Just Like Dad 47

Chapter 7: In the Mist 57

Chapter 8: Panic 65

Chapter 9: Chicken and Biscuits Again 71

Chapter 10: No Room for Harry 79

About the Author 85

About the Illustrator 87

Also by Lisa Reinicke 88

CHAPTER ONE

A SMOKING EGG

Beep, beep, beep! Beep, beep, beep!

Harry, the hairy troll, opened his sleepy eyes but could not see anything. "What is that noise? It must stop!" Harry grumped, covering his big ears with his hands.

But the noise did not stop.

Beep, beep, beep! Beep, beep, beep!

"A r g h ! "

Harry rubbed off goopy pieces of sleep stuck to his old troll eyelids. He wiped them out of the corners of his eyes with his fat finger. Circles of dark grey smoke filled his stone cave.

Harry jumped out of bed. When his giant feet hit the cold stone floor, his toes curled. October mornings were always chilly in Norway.

"Brrr," Harry said with a shake. He looked at Piff, his dragon. Piff was huddled under the covers, sleeping through the loud beeping of the smoke alarm.

Harry had lived a happy, quiet life as a hermit until Piff came along. Life was easier alone. Piff was a lot of trouble. But the young pink dragon was family now. And somehow life was better.

Their cave home was tucked into the side of a hill covered with green grass. Many other trolls, fairies, and elves lived nearby in the forest.

Piff woke up and started crying. Harry needed to get Piff away from the smoke.

"Whaaaaaaaaaaa, whaaaaaaaa!" Little Piff was shaking. She jumped into Harry's arms. Harry pulled her close, knowing she must be scared.

"Whaaaaaaaaa, whaaaaaaaaa!" Piff cried again. A bit of snot dripped from her snout into Harry's ear.

"Hush, Piff," Harry scolded, wiping his ear. "I need to think." The smoke made Harry cough. "We must find our breakfast egg in the kitchen. Then, we need to get out of the cave until the smoke clears."

Piff nodded through her tears.

She liked eggs and toast just as much as Harry did.

When they got to the smoke-filled kitchen, they both heard a strange sound.

"Puffffffffff! Puffffffffffff!"

It sounded like a balloon being untied and released.

Harry held Piff closer, giving her a gentle pat.

"Pufffffffffff! Puffffff!" The sound was now louder.

The room smelled like dirty socks. Piff buried her snout in the troll's shirt and sneezed.

"Yuck!" Harry said. "What is that terrible smell?"

Beep, beep, beep! The smoke alarm continued.

"Whaaaaaaaaaaaaaaaaaaa, whaaaaaaaaaa!" Piff cried.

"Puffffffffff! Puffffffffffff!" The sound came from behind the smelly smoke.

"All this noise is driving me crazy!" Harry shouted. "Make it stop!"

Suddenly, a small blue figure appeared in the smoke.

Harry's mouth fell open. He almost dropped Piff on the floor.

Piff stopped crying and clawed Harry's suspenders with her sharp nails. The troll's baggy pants fell to his knees.

"Puuuffffffff! Puuffffff," the little blue creature snorted again, pushing smoke out of its snout. Pieces of blue speckled eggshell covered its head and the floor. Its green eyes peered out through

the smoke. Harry thought they looked like emeralds.

"Piff-scared." The dragon held Harry tighter. Her pink wings were shaking.

As the smoke began to clear, a toothless smile appeared. Harry and Piff looked more closely at the small smoking creature.

"Oh, no! Not again!" Harry slapped his forehead. "Another breakfast egg has turned into a dragon! What am I to do with another dragon?"

CHAPTER
TWO

YAY TO STAY!

The smoke alarms finally stopped beeping. Harry could think again.

He decided the new dragon must be a boy. Its horns were different from Piff's. Her horns curved while the blue dragon's horns went straight back.

Harry studied the blue dragon and began to pace. The small blue creature looked up sadly with its big green eyes.

"Oh, no, you don't." The troll covered his eyes with his giant hands. "No, no, no! Listen here, dragon, you are very cute...but there is no room for you in my cave. You cannot stay, not even one day! One, two, three, out the door with thee!"

The blue dragon shook like a wet dog. Eggshell pieces crackled across the cave's stone floor.

"See what I mean?" the troll shouted. "All little dragons do is make messes. Too much work! Too much to do.

One dragon. Two dragons. One must ***skiddoo***."

Harry got the broom and dustpan from the closet and began to sweep.

While Harry cleaned up, Piff tiptoed over and licked the chubby new whelp across the chin.

"Puuuuuufffff! Puffffffffffff!" the blue dragon wheezed, spouting out more smelly smoke.

The smoke siren beeped a warning chime.

Harry looked up and frowned. But then he saw the two dragons sitting side by side, blinking at each other. One was a small, pink **fledgling** with sparkling blue eyes with long lashes. She had beautiful wings and small horns that curved. The other was a short, stocky blue whelp with sad, emerald green eyes. He had long horns that went straight back. His wings were almost too big for his body. He needed to grow into them. He had a sweet, crooked, toothless smile that Harry tried to ignore.

The troll chuckled at the sight. Harry crossed his arms and tapped his foot. Tap, tap, tap. He rubbed his chin whiskers.

While Harry liked being alone, he loved Piff. Yes, she made a lot of messes, but she was fun. He had grown used to being with her. She made life better. The two had a comfortable routine. Harry liked routines. He liked things the same. Change was not easy for an old troll.

"Hurumpf," Harry stomped, "Okay, little blue dragon, you can stay...but only for one day. And I'll have no trouble from either of you, understand?"

Both dragons' tails began to beat the floor happily. They looked at each other and smiled. Their tails beat the floor even harder.

Craaaaack! The blue dragon's

overactive tail hit a kitchen chair. Two legs broke off and smacked down on the stone floor.

"Argh!" Harry grumbled, pulling on his rainbow-colored hair. "You've broken my chair!"

The blue dragon waddled over with his head hanging and started to pick up the pieces.

Harry calmed down. "So, I see you're a helper." He patted the stocky dragon. "Well, at least you're good for something, lil fella."

Harry grabbed some glue and sat on the floor. His hairy legs creaked when he crossed them to sit. His pants slipped down in the back to show the crack at the top of his bottom. Piff snickered. Harry started to put the chair back together. The young boy dragon plopped down beside him and watched. Piff came over to watch, too. Their eyes followed Harry's every move. Back and forth. Up and down. Once the super-strong trolligan glue dried, Harry got up off the floor.

"Well, you two are a fine pair of trouble," Harry complained as he worked.

Both dragons looked at each other and nodded their heads up and down in a secret sibling language.

Harry scratched his chin. He knew the two dragons would soon be getting into all kinds of trouble together.

---

fledgling (fledg·ling) noun—a young bird or dragon
skiddoo (ski·doo) verb—to go away or get out

CHAPTER THREE

MANNERS AND MUNCHIES

Harry was hungry. "No eggs," he complained, "and one more mouth to feed. No eggs for breakfast. No eggs for lunch. No eggs tomorrow, but that's just a ***hunch***."

He went to the cupboard and took out a loaf of bread and a stick of butter.

"Toast it is then." Harry began buttering

the bread. "One pat here, one pat there. Do that twice, and that's a square." He tapped his foot. He was very pleased with his new rhyme.

The two dragons inched their way toward the table. Their small talons clicked with each move.

"Piff," Harry said. "What should we call our guest?"

The little blue dragon started thumping his tail but stopped when he remembered breaking the chair. The dragon rubbed his hungry blue tummy and made tiny puffing noises. With each sound, a small plume of smoke escaped from his ***snout***.

"Puff," said Piff.

"Puff?" asked Harry. "That dragon sure puffs out a lot of smelly smoke for such a wee creature."

"Puff," said Piff again.

Harry laughed. "Puff it is then. Puff and Piff."

Piff smiled and nodded her pink head up and down. The blue dragon nodded his head, too.

"Now that you have a name," Harry continued, "I suppose you both are hungry? All I have is toast."

Harry went back to buttering the toast. Before he could finish, Puff grabbed the bread out of Harry's hand and swallowed it in one gulp.

"No, Puff," Harry scolded. "That's bad manners." Piff sat quietly and shook her head back and forth.

"Listen, little Puff," Harry began to rhyme, "a pat of butter is my task.

I'll make your toast, and make it fast, but..."

The hungry blue dragon snorted another puff of smelly smoke and grabbed the bread from Harry's hand again.

Harry gritted his teeth. "No, Puff! We have manners in this cave! You don't grab food. You must wait your turn."

When Harry turned to make more toast, the blue dragon pulled the whole loaf down to the floor and shook his head back and forth. Chunks of bread flew from his full mouth. He was gulping down the bread and hardly chewing.

Piff pushed the new dragon out of the way to get a few bites of crust. "P-grrrr!" She wrinkled up her snout and squinted her eyes.

Smoke billowed from the blue

dragon's nostrils. He pushed Piff away and growled back.

Yelping and screeching in a swirl of dark grey smoke, the two dragons pulled, pushed, and growled. The smoke siren started to blare again. Beep, beep, beep. Smoke began to fill the cave. White bread crumbs were all over the floor. The mess looked like snow.

Harry stood over the two dragons, watching them fight. He shook his head and wondered how a simple breakfast could get so out of hand.

"Stop right now! Both of you," Harry yelled. "I want quiet!"

The dragons stopped fighting and looked at Harry.

The hairy troll opened the cave window to let out the smoke.

The cave siren stopped blaring.

Harry slumped down on the stone floor under the window. He covered his eyes with his big hands. He bowed his head and tucked his hairy knees into his chest.

Piff thought Harry might be crying. She scooted over and gave him a big lick across the chin.

"Piff-sorry."

Harry wiped off the slobber with the back of his hand and gave her a small pat on the head. Puff waddled over to Harry and snorted warm, smelly smoke. He nuzzled under Harry's big arm.

Harry looked at the mess in his cave. It was still morning, but he was already tired. He looked at the two sorry little dragons. "Hmpf," was all Harry could say.

Harry stood up, tightening his suspenders, and began to clean. He swept the crumbs into a pile. Both dragons used their tails to help.

Harry stopped cleaning and looked at Puff. "If you're going to stay, you will need to have manners, understood?"

Puff nodded.

"And there will be no more fighting, you two, understood?"

"Piff-promise."

Puff nodded in agreement.

"Go sit in the corner, you two troublemakers. I need to finish cleaning."

Piff and Puff hugged each other and went to the corner. They sat close together, smiling.

"No good can come from keeping dragons," Harry muttered while he cleaned.

The dragons began licking their lips. Piff started whimpering. "Piff-hungry. Piff-food."

In a moment, Piff was at a full scream, and Puff was at a roar. These two small dragons were getting ***hangry***.

---

hunch (hunch) noun—a strong feeling that something is going to happen.

snout (snaut) noun—a long nose, usually on an animal's face.
hangry (han·gree) adjective—so hungry you are getting angry.

CHAPTER
FOUR

MARCHING ONWARD

In the hills and mountains of Norway, people leave out food for trolls. The Norwegian people believe happy, well-fed trolls bring good luck. Hungry, grumpy trolls play tricks. Harry liked this belief because he enjoyed free food.

Goat farmers left goat cheese and sausage. Sheep farmers offered lamb chops and sheep cheese. If Harry were lucky today, someone would leave a few fresh eggs—without

dragons inside! Now that Harry knew what dragon eggs looked like, he would not be fooled again.

"We need some food." Harry looked at his two hungry dragons. Their tails started twirling and made a humming sound. He grabbed his backpack, then realized he needed two more bags.

The young dragons watched as Harry took two square cloths and tied the ends together. He asked the dragons to go out into the yard and find two long sticks.

"And there will be no arguing," Harry scolded. "Bring the sticks back to me quickly. We're all hungry."

The dragons were back with the sticks in two minutes. Harry slid one stick through each fabric bag he'd made. He handed one bag to each dragon.

"Carry the stick over your shoulder

with the bag in the back," Harry instructed. The two dragons tried their bags on for size. Harry thought they looked like ***hobos***.

"Ready?" Harry asked. "Let's walk through the forest and up to the farms to find some food." The troll led the way. Behind him, Piff marched proudly, her tail wagging.

Puff did not look as confident. He was pouting and shuffling his feet. The little blue dragon let out a frustrated "Puufffff" each time his bag fell off his shoulder and hit the dirt.

Harry felt bad for Puff. "Hold on to the end of the stick and stop dragging your feet."

Puff still kept dropping his bag. By now, a big angry billow of smoke followed the dragon.

"Come on. You can do it, Puff," Harry urged him.

For the next twenty minutes, everything went smoothly. Then, Piff tripped on a root and fell down face first in the dirt.

"Piff-ouch!" She whined. "Too haaard." She stayed face down and played dead.

"Too haaard!" Puff panted.

"Now, now, you two lazybones. At home, you both have enough energy to fight and squabble. You roll around on the floor. Now you don't have the energy to walk? That won't do. Get moving. We are almost there."

Harry picked up the pink dragon and gave her a love pat on the back. She whined but started walking again.

"Puff," Harry encouraged, "up you go, buddy." Harry helped set Puff's bag back in place. He gave the blue dragon a pat on the top of his head.

Harry was in a good mood because there would be plenty of free food for them at the farms. He began to sing a little march.

"Left foot once. Left foot twice. Right foot three times, makes things nice." Harry marched as he sang.

The dragons also stepped in time until they reached the farms. There, they found lots of food. Harry put at least a dozen eggs into Piff's pouch. He packed the pouch with grass to keep the eggs from breaking. "A nest for our eggs, to keep them safe," Harry told the dragons. Then, he wrapped them snugly with his ***kerchief*** to keep them from rattling against each other.

Sausage and cheese went into Puff's pouch. At one cottage, the troll found twenty pancakes wrapped in a towel. "Today is a very good day," Harry smiled. There was lots of fried chicken, too.

"Yum!" cried Harry. "We shall have crispy fried chicken and buttered biscuits today with lots and lots of butter!"

After they had filled their sacks with troll food, Harry picked some carrots, yams, and turnips from the farmers' fields. This would please the farmers who believed a well-fed troll was a happy troll.

"It's time to go home." Harry began to sing his march again. "Left foot once. Left foot twice. Right foot three times, makes things nice."

A short distance down the trail, Harry picked some ***cloudberries***, the crown jewel of Norwegian fruits. They

looked like large, orange-pink raspberries and tasted like candy. He also found arctic blueberries and wheatgrass. Puff and Piff picked even more berries than Harry. Finally, Harry gathered a few delicious almonds and hazelnuts.

"Piff-tired," the pink dragon whimpered.

"Puff-tired," the blue dragon slumped.

The exhausted pair shuffled slowly behind Harry. They were both so tired, they dropped their bags filled with food.

Harry went back and picked up their bags. At this rate, he wondered if they would ever get home. The hairy troll was hungry and tired, too. Mostly, he was tired of dealing with little dragons.

---

hobo (ho·bo) noun—a poor traveling worker.
kerchief (ker•chief) noun—a square cloth used as a head covering or worn as a scarf around the neck.
cloudberry (cloud·ber·ree) noun—a creeping plant in the raspberry family. It produces an edible, amber-colored fruit.

CHAPTER
FIVE

His bottom lip was hitting against his tusks with each breath. Piff noticed Harry's dirty fingers and had an idea. She took colored berries and started painting Harry's nails.

She was very careful and quiet. Every so often, Harry would shake and jerk as he inhaled. "Ouuukkk... hu...hu...hu... ouuukkk." Piff giggled quietly and kept painting. Finally, Harry's fingernails were all the colors of the rainbow.

Puff purred and giggled, too, pushing tiny clouds of smoke out of his snout. He took his berries and began to paint the troll's toenails.

"Pretty," Piff whispered.

"Puurrrrrfffect," Puff said quietly.

After the two dragons admired their work, they went back to coloring.

Piff traced her foot on the paper and painted a pretty ring on one toe.

Puff was not so neat. He scribbled the page in every color.

Puff looked at his drawing and then at Piff's. He frowned and snorted a big stinky cloud of smoke. He did not like his drawing. He threw down his paper and stomped on it. Then he crossed his arms and sat right on top of Piff's artwork.

Piff started bawling. "Baahhh, baahhh. Waaaaa, waaaaa." She pushed Puff off her artwork and hissed. Puff tumbled into Harry's chair, waking up the snoring troll.

"Whaaa...whaa...?" Harry shook his sleepy head and wiped the drool from his lips. "What is going on here?"

A very unhappy Harry stood and picked up the two dragons by the scruff of their necks. Holding Piff in his right hand and Puff in his left, he dangled the dragons in midair. Legs moving and wings flapping, they both continued to hiss.

"Why can't you two get along? Why are you fighting now?" Harry's voice was loud and grumpy.

Piff pointed at her picture and started crying again.

Puff blew a big cloud of smoke right into Harry's face.

"Puff, if you make the cave siren go off again, you are going to be in big trouble. Calm down right now, little man."

Puff growled under his breath and held in his smoke.

"What started this?" Harry asked.

Piff pointed to Puff's crumpled drawing and then to her artwork.

"Humph," the troll said. "Puff, you are jealous. The green monster, I call it. Jealousy is no good. You need to do your best work. You need to mind your temper. You can't throw a fit every time someone does something better than you."

Harry put both dragons down. He

continued to scold, pointing at both drawings with his big troll hands.

Both dragons began to giggle.

"This is not funny. No more fighting, understood?"

The dragons were not paying attention. Harry was frustrated.

"You cannot hit and push!" He waved his hands above his head and began to stomp his feet, trying to get the two dragons to listen.

Both dragons burst out laughing. Harry's colored fingernails and toenails were too funny. The dragons were laughing so hard they had to hold their bellies with their claws.

Harry looked at his toenails and fingernails and gasped. They were all painted different colors. Purple, green, red, orange, and yellow nails swept side to side as he spoke

"Grrrrrrr. I have no peace!" Harry was angry and hungry. He was hangry. He stomped off to the kitchen to find some lunch. Food would make them all feel better.

CHAPTER
SIX

JUST LIKE DAD

Harry sliced sausage and goat cheese. He put them on the table with some bread. All the delicious food put him in a better mood.

Harry popped two pieces of cheese into his mouth and began to sing. "One slice, two slice, three slice, four.

Five slice, six slice, seven not more." He popped another slice of cheese into his mouth and smiled. "Eight and nine slices are all mine! Trolls need food to feel just fine!"

Harry added the fresh crispy fried chicken and buttery biscuits to the feast. His mouth was watering as he set the plates on the table. He called for the two dragons. "Come in here, you naughty little dragons. It's time for lunch." Both dragons ran into the kitchen and hopped up on the same chair at the same time. Puff's robust rump knocked Piff off.

Piff jumped back up and pushed Puff off the chair. "Piff-mine!" she screeched as Puff tumbled to the floor.

Puff growled and let out a stream of smoke. His emerald eyes narrowed.

Harry frowned, crossed his arms,

and showed his big front tusk. "There will be no more fighting," he growled. "It's time for lunch and for some quiet. Besides, isn't it time we started acting like a family?"

Piff and Puff blinked. They looked at Harry and then at each other. No one said a word. Then Piff hugged Puff.

"Piff-happy."

Puff hugged his new big sister. "Puff-happy."

Harry smiled and put meat, cheese, carrots, chicken, and biscuits on each of their plates. The little dragons ate everything in seconds.

Piff started crunching on a carrot. Chomp, chomp, chomp.

"Piff-ouch!" She spit out a piece of carrot on her plate. Right in the middle was a small, white, pointy tooth.

"Oh, no!" Harry cried, putting his

hands to his face, "What have I done? I have fed you something bad for dragons, and now you're coming apart!"

He ran to get *Good Dragons of the Woods*. It was his guide to taking care of dragons. Turning pages, he looked for dragon teeth. He wanted to know if Piff would die without her tooth. He kept skimming until he found the information he needed.

He read the book out loud. "Dragons are delivered in an eggshell." This, Harry knew. "The whelp (baby dragon) breaks open the shell when it's strong enough. The baby uses an egg tooth to crack open the shell. This is called pipping. The whelp loses the egg tooth shortly after as it grows into a fledgling."

Puff felt his snout to see if he had an egg tooth. He did, which made him smile.

"Thank goodness," Harry said, wrapping Piff's tooth in a tissue and placing it on the kitchen counter. Harry had heard that the forest fairies gathered teeth at night and left treats. Sometimes other hidden people, called ***Huldufólk***, helped the fairies. He hoped they would come for Piff's tooth and leave her a nice treat.

"Let's have dessert," Harry said. Both dragons beat their tails happily, but not too hard. They didn't want to break any more chairs.

The dragons watched as Harry put the berries in a bowl and squashed them. He then added a small amount of brown goat-milk cream. In Norway, brown goat cheese is called ***Gjetost***. *Yay-toast* is how you say the word. It is as sweet as caramel and as thick as fudge.

Harry put the cheese and berries on the pancakes and took a bite. "Yum!" He took another bite. "Yuuummmm!" When he took his third taste, he danced around in a circle. "Yummmmy!" Piff and Puff both let out a whine. They had drool dripping from their mouths as they waited.

"Patience." Harry started another one of his rhymes. "One pancake flat. Add cheese with a pat. Berries go splat. Fold in half like that." Harry hopped from one foot to the other as he sang. "Makes a troll plenty fat." He smiled and took another big bite of the folded pancake. Cream rolled down his chin. The dragons watched and drooled even more.

Harry gave each dragon one pancake with cheese and berries on top. Piff and Puff ate their dessert in one bite and asked for more.

"Nay, my little dragons, no more today. Maybe tomorrow. I don't want you to get tummy aches."

Harry smiled. He was starting to sound like his dad, Hairy, the hairy troll. Harry loved sweets when he was a small troll. His parents were always worried he would get a tummy ache or cavities. Harry still loved sweets.

"Humph, a parent I can be!" He patted his full, happy stomach and looked over at the dragons. To his surprise, his two feisty monsters were holding hands. Well, would you look at that, he thought. What a fine day it has been.

But Harry worried that tomorrow might bring more problems. Caring for two dragons was turning out to be a big job for an old troll.

Huldufólk (hull·de·foke) noun—hidden people in Icelandic folklore. Supernatural beings who live in forests and caves. Trolls, elves, and fairies are Huldufólk.

Gjetost (yay·toast) noun—type of brown goat cheese made from whey, the liquid left over from curdled milk. The whey is boiled for hours to form the cheese.

CHAPTER
SEVEN

IN THE MIST

Puff went to the front door and sat down. "Puff-out," he grunted with a small burst of smoke.

"You want to go outside?" Harry asked.

"Puff-out." The young dragon wagged his tail.

The old troll thought about the dangers in the forest. He shivered at the thought of Puff being outside alone.

Harry scratched the back of his head under his man bun.

"Do you want to play outside?" he asked Puff.

The dragon nodded.

"Piff, you come, too." Harry pointed at the pink fledgling. His finger swung from the dragon to the door.

The two dragons ran out, almost knocking him over on the way.

Puff ran outside first. Piff stopped outside the doorway. She looked at Harry and blinked her eyes.

"It's okay, Piff," Harry said. "Go play."

Harry tried to stay calm. He couldn't keep the young dragons inside forever. But they knew nothing about the dangers of the forest.

"On second thought," the troll said, "let's go for a walk. You must stay where I can see you. Better yet, stay where you can see me."

The trio set off on their walk. They

entered one of Harry's favorite places for a stroll, the Vidden Trail. It wove through the nearby hills and mountains. The trail was clearly marked and well-worn by both trolls and grazing sheep. The sound of sheep bells filled the air. Green grass grew on either side of the trail. Small animals like red squirrels, foxes, and rabbits hid in the grass and sometimes crossed the trail.

Harry found a walking stick, which he used to help him step over rocks along the path. The two dragons ran ahead, eager to play.

"Piff-happy!" the pink dragon yelled joyfully at the top of her lungs. Her voice echoed through the hills.

"Puff-happy!" the blue dragon let out a trail of smoke and waited to hear his echo, too.

Their two tails wagged together as they hopped and jumped back and forth on the trail. Everyone was happy. "My hermit life is not to be," Harry smiled. "Now noisy dragons bring me glee."

As they walked, Harry kept an eye out for *cairns*. These trail markers were stacks of stones that made a map to follow if you got lost.

A light rain started to fall. Harry knew that storms popped up quickly here. He could hear thunder in the distance. He had let the dragons wander together on the trail. Now, he had lost sight of them. He could hear heavier rain coming from around the next hill.

"Piff? Puff? Where are you two?" Harry called out. He heard his echo, but no reply from the dragons. He tried to walk faster, but the trail was muddy. His big feet got stuck and slowed him down.

He was worried about his dragons.

"Piff! Puff!" Harry shouted over and over again. The old troll was panting and soaking wet. The rain was coming down harder. Harry could only see a few feet in front of his face. His man bun drooped to the base of his neck. Slippery rocks caused him to stumble.

"Piff!! Puff!!" he yelled again at the top of his lungs. "Where are you?" Harry only heard his echo and the rain.

Then, from somewhere distant in the valley, he heard a loud "Screeeechhh! Aaaaiiiieeee!" Harry ran toward the sound as fast as he could.

CHAPTER
EIGHT

PANIC

Harry's heart was pounding. "Please, oh please, keep my dragons safe until I find them!"

"Screeeechhh! Aaaaiiiieeee!" The cry came again.

Check your surroundings, you silly old troll, Harry thought. *Look for signs.* At the base of the North Mountain, Harry noticed a grey cloud circling in the misty rain.

"Smoke!" Harry yelled. He started to run. "Puff's smoke! I see Puff's smoke! Stay where you are, Piff and Puff. I'm coming." But Harry knew the dragons could not hear him.

The troll curled his lips and whistled as loud as he could.

Harry whistled a second time even louder, but there was no answer. The rings of smoke were gone.

Harry fell to his knees.

"Oh, no! What has happened to my poor dragons? They are lost!" The troll closed his eyes, fell to his knees in the mud, and began to cry. He was sure something terrible had happened.

Then, Harry felt a warm snort of air on the back of his neck. The troll stayed very still and kept his eyes closed. The monster that ate my little dragons has come to eat me, he thought. A second, stronger snort blew Harry's man bun. The troll waited to be eaten by the monster.

Something nudged him from behind. “Piiiiiiiiiff!” Grey smoke circled the troll’s head. Harry felt something lick his ear. He lifted his head and peeked through his arms. There was no beast or monster—only two wet dragons.

“You’re alive! You are both here! You are not dead!” Harry scrambled to his feet and hugged the two dragons with his big, hairy arms.

“Pifouhhhhh,” Piff squealed and licked Harry’s whole face.

“Oh, and you too, Puff! I thought you were both gone for good,” Harry said.

Puff blew smelly smoke in the troll's face. Usually this would annoy Harry, but today it made him smile. He hugged the chubby dragon.

Harry was so happy to see his two little dragons. Then he remembered how they had run off and made him so scared.

"I have a good mind to leave you both here in the forest. What were you thinking, running off like that? Humph, you two are in big trouble."

But Harry didn't have the energy to stay mad at them. He turned and started back down the path, looking for the cairns that marked the way.

Piff hung her head and followed the troll.

Puff waddled close behind his sister.

"Come on, you two," Harry ordered. "Let's get back to the cave."

STOP when you have a problem

S is for stop. Stop what you are doing for a minute.
T is for think. Think about what you can do or need to do.
O is for observe. Look around you for safe places or signs.
P is for plan. Plan what you should do next.

CHAPTER NINE

CHICKEN AND BISCUITS AGAIN

Muddy, tired, and grumpy, the trio arrived back at the cave. The dragons pushed the door open.

Each dragon wanted to be the first to go inside. Puff pushed Piff out of the way and raced ahead. His feet were covered with mud. Now the floor was a mess.

Harry groaned when he saw the mud and told both dragons to go to the kitchen and sit down. "Stay right there and don't move a muscle!"

Harry went to another room and

brought back a wet towel. He started cleaning the mud from the dragons' feet.

"I hate messes!" Harry scolded. "Do not come into our cave with muddy paws again. Do you understand?"

"Now, it's time to clean the floor," Harry instructed. "Grab a towel and get to work." The three worked for almost an hour cleaning all the floors.

"Good work. Now you understand why I get tired and grumpy when you two get in fights and make messes. It's a lot of work to clean them up. But you were both a big help. Cleaning is faster when we all work together. Many hands make little work!" Harry said.

"Now, go lie down so I can get some food ready for our dinner. Do not fight. Do not make any messes. Do not push. Do not whine. Do not make a peep until dinner." He wagged his finger at the two as he spoke.

Piff scratched the ground. She circled her body around and around to find a soft spot to sit. Puff plopped down on the floor. He stretched out his chubby body, unable to curl into a ball. Both dragons placed their heads on a front leg and closed their eyes, drifting off for a nap. Their chests rose and fell with each breath. Piff tucked her tail under her bottom. Puff's tail sprawled across the floor.

Harry sighed and went to the kitchen to start cooking.

Fried chicken with biscuits was Harry's favorite meal. He was tired, but the thought of chicken and biscuits for dinner put him in a better mood.

"Chicken and biscuits make my day. One piece, two piece, that's the way. Some for dragons, more for me. Chicken and biscuits, oh, yippee!" he sang.

The smell of fresh biscuits filled the cave, waking both dragons from their nap. The fledglings stretched and yawned.

Harry watched the dragons walk into the kitchen. They both looked bigger. Have my two dragons grown? he wondered.

He put two pieces of chicken and five biscuits on each of their plates. In a few seconds, all the food was gone. Harry's dragons were *very* hungry. The pair looked at the troll's plate, drooling for more.

"Oh, no, you don't! That's for me," Harry warned and gave them the leftover pancakes and berries. Finally, the dragons seemed full.

Harry finished his chicken and biscuits and asked the dragons to help him clean. Neither dragon moved. Harry thought it might be time for "the rules" talk that his mother had given him when he was just a wee little troll.

"You two come here," Harry motioned, pointing at the couch.

"Now that there are three of us sharing this cave, it's time to review the Dragon Rules. First, no pushing and no fighting. Second, don't go out of my sight when you are outside. Third, no messes. If you make a mess, clean it up. Fourth, you will help find and carry food without complaining."

Both dragons beat their tails on the floor. Puff blew smoke in Harry's face. Piff licked the troll's chin.

"Fifth, no licking!" The troll wiped his chin and grinned.

"Now, off to the bathtub with both of you, and then it's time for bed!" The dragons started pushing each other to see who could get to the tub first. They had already forgotten Harry's rules.

CHAPTER TEN

NO ROOM FOR HARRY

Piff loved bath time. She splashed and played in the water. She looked like a pink duck diving into a lake.

Puff did *not* like bath time. He sat on the bathroom floor, shivering. Harry tried to pick Puff up to put him in the water. The dragon's tiny claws gripped the bathroom rug. The more the troll pulled, the more the dragon dug into the carpet.

"Puff, you have to take a bath," Harry said. "Don't be scared. See how much fun Piff is having?"

The troll pulled Puff off the carpet. He placed the blue dragon in the water. Puff splashed and blew big streams of smelly smoke. He flapped his wings back and forth wildly, sending water all over the bathroom floor.

Piff splashed Puff in the face, giggling. Puff coughed, sneezed, and yelled.

Harry scrubbed Puff with soap and rinsed him off. Then he plucked him from the water.

He dried the blue fledgling with a towel. The dragon

shook the leftover drops of water onto the floor.

Piff giggled more. She dove under the water again and again. She was more like a mermaid than a dragon.

Harry grabbed her between dives. Then dried her off. "Dry and clean," Harry said. "It's time for bed."

Piff jumped into her spot in the troll's bed and wiggled under the blanket. Her head found the soft pillow. Puff tried to follow but missed. His booty fell back onto the floor.

Piff giggled. Puff blew smoke.

"No more smoke today, Puff, " Harry said, lifting the blue dragon onto the bed.

Harry looked at the bed full of dragons. There was no room for a troll.

Stomping to the closet, he got

extra blankets and a pillow. They would make a good sleeping bag.

Harry noticed the dragons had their arms around each other. Piff was pretending to read *Good Dragons of the Woods* to Puff.

"Ppp, p, ppp, pp, p, pppp, ppppiff," she mouthed confidently.

"Silly little dragons," Harry smiled.

The troll went back to the kitchen to

get Piff's egg tooth. He hid it in his hand while he said goodnight. He then patted each fledgling on the head and gently slipped the egg tooth under Piff's pillow.

Harry turned off the light and got into his sleeping bag. It felt good to lie down. He loved his two mischievous dragons, but they wore him out. He stared out his bedroom window and thought about the day. All in all, it was a good day. A breeze came through the window, and Harry saw a flash of light. Probably just lightning from a far-off storm, he thought. Or maybe a fairy was coming for Piff's egg tooth. He couldn't be sure.

As he drifted off to sleep, he sang, "I'm just a

hermit in my cave. Eggs for breakfast is all I crave."

His lips curled in a small smile as he finished his song. "Now two little dragons live with this troll. Piff and Puff, my heart you stole."

Harry was happy, a strange feeling for a grumpy troll.

He blew a kiss toward the bed, closed his eyes, and fell asleep. Harry's snores drifted out into the night. Another flash of light came through the bedroom window, hinting at what tomorrow might bring.

ABOUT THE AUTHOR

Author **Lisa Reinicke** loves dragonflies and has won many of them. She has received the Purple Dragonfly award for several books, including *Bart's Escape Out the Gate*, *Wilhelmina's Wish*, and *Wings and Feet*. Some other shiny awards are Book Excellence, Mom's Choice, and Readers' Favorite. In 2019, she added a Benjamin Franklin Award to the collection. She loves to tell stories and has created more than 35 of them for local TV and audio recordings. Telling whoppers is her business.

All of her books are entertaining yet focus on social issues that engage children and parents in discussion. Lisa works passionately raising money and donating her time to charities that improve children's lives physically, emotionally, and spiritually.

Website: LisaReinicke.com
Facebook: www.facebook.com/lisareinickeauthor
Twitter: @lisarauthor
Instagram: @lisareinicke_author
YouTube: Lisa Reinicke on YouTube

ABOUT THE ILLUSTRATOR

Analise Black began her career as a character designer and discovered her love for children's books. She now works as a full-time children's book illustrator. Using traditional and digital media, Analise creates worlds where a child's imagination can journey. She lives in Colorado with her family and her beloved cat, Catnis. Follow Analise on Instagram @analiseblack_ and visit her website at analiseblack.com.

ALSO BY LISA REINICKE

Harry's Dragon Tales
Toast with a Side of Dragon (grades K-2)

Arnold: The Cute Little Pig with Personality (ages 2-6)
Wings and Feet (grades K-2)
Wings and Feet Activity Book (grades K-2)
David's Christmas Wish: A Timeless Christmas Story (all ages)
Bart's Escape Out the Gate (ages 3-7)
Wilhelmina's Wish (ages 3-7)

Made in the USA
Middletown, DE
13 April 2021